POINT GUARD
PRIDE

BY JAKE MADDOX

text by
Salima Alikhan

STONE ARCH BOOKS
a capstone imprint

Jake Maddox JV is published by Stone Arch Books, an imprint of Capstone.
1710 Roe Crest Drive
North Mankato, Minnesota 56003
www.capstonepub.com

Library of Congress Cataloging-in-Publication Data
Names: Maddox, Jake, author.
Title: Point guard pride / Jake Maddox; text by Salima Alikhan
Description: North Mankato, Minnesota : Stone Arch Books, an imprint of Capstone, [2021] |
Series: Jake Maddox JV girls | Audience: Ages 8-11. | Audience: Grades 4-6. |
Summary: Twelve-year-old Yasmin, a talented point guard on her school basketball team,
learns about teamwork and standing up for oneself when she experiences racism at her new
middle school.
Identifiers: LCCN 2020035121 (print) | LCCN 2020035122 (ebook) | ISBN 9781515882350
(library binding) | ISBN 9781515883463 (paperback) | ISBN 9781515892175 (pdf)
Subjects: CYAC: Basketball—Fiction. | Racism—Fiction. | Teamwork (Sports)—Fiction. |
Middle schools—Fiction. | Schools—Fiction. | Racially mixed people—Fiction.
Classification: LCC PZ7.M25643 Pq 2021 (print) | LCC PZ7.M25643 (ebook) | DDC [Fic]—
dc23
LC record available at https://lccn.loc.gov/2020035121
LC ebook record available at https://lccn.loc.gov/2020035122

Designer: Dina Her

Image Credits:
Shutterstock: Brocreative, design element, Dmytro Surkov, Cover, Eky Studio, design
element, Isniper, design element, taka1022, design element throughout

Printed and bound in the USA. PO 3837

TABLE OF CONTENTS

CHAPTER 1
THREE-POINT JONES......................**5**

CHAPTER 2
NOT IN HOUSTON ANYMORE................**13**

CHAPTER 3
MAKING A PLAN...........................**23**

CHAPTER 4
READY TO CONQUER.......................**33**

CHAPTER 5
SLAYING AT PRACTICE....................**39**

CHAPTER 6
DEALING AT DINNER......................**47**

CHAPTER 7
THE DANCE..............................**51**

CHAPTER 8
DEFEAT.................................**59**

CHAPTER 9
PLAYING IT SMART.......................**67**

CHAPTER 10
TELLING...............................**73**

CHAPTER 11
TEAMWORK..............................**81**

CHAPTER 1

THREE-POINT JONES

Yasmin Jones tore around the court, sneakers squeaking on the gym floor, the crowd roaring in her ears. It was the last quarter of Dexter Middle School's basketball game. The score was neck and neck, 22–20, with their rival middle school, Greendale, in the lead.

It was also Yasmin's first game for Dexter. She was determined to show Coach that he'd been smart to let her start at point guard. At her old school, they'd called her Three-Point Jones for her famous three-pointers—the best in the region.

"I'm open!" shouted Kelly Holgar, Dexter's shooting guard. Small, fast, and blond, she zipped past the other players down the court.

Yasmin stayed near the three-point line. If one of her teammates managed to get possession and pass to her, she'd make the shot that would get them ahead by a point—she was sure of it.

The Greendale team was good—passing back and forth at lightning speed, moving the ball down the court quickly. Late in the game, Yasmin managed to block one of Greendale's shots, timing and positioning her block perfectly.

As she took possession of the ball, she heard Coach shouting, "Yes! Go, Yasmin!" She tore down the court, beaming. Coach was noticing her game.

The Greendale girl guarding her was good. But Yasmin was catching her off guard by staying low with her dribbles. She was good at changing speed and direction when she had the ball. But she switched hands on a spin move, which opened her up for the

Greendale girl to steal the ball. Greendale was back in possession.

Heidi Schultz, Dexter's center and the tallest girl on the team, stole the ball back on Greendale's pass, her strawberry-blond hair flying behind her. Yasmin cheered—they were in possession again.

She shouted that she was open, but Heidi passed to Kelly, who saw an opening and went to shoot a layup. The shot clanked off the rim, but Kelly got the rebound. Dexter still had possession. Kelly was looking toward the hoop and not behind her at the three-point line, where Yasmin was.

"I'm *open!*" Yasmin shouted. She just had to get her hands on that ball.

Finally, Kelly heard her, pivoted, and passed. Yasmin caught the ball, took a deep breath, and focused in on the basket. She took the shot. The soaring glory of her famous three-pointer sailed through the air—and went clean through the net. A perfect shot!

The Dexter crowd went wild. There were only five seconds left in the game—not enough time for the Greendale Giants to recover. Dexter was walking away with a win!

Yasmin jumped up and down with the rest of her team. Winning her first game for Dexter would *definitely* earn her a place on the team, and at the school. No other twelve-year-old could shoot three-pointers like she did—they didn't call her Three-Point Jones for nothing.

Still feeling like she was walking on air, she went back to the locker room. She was pulling her towel out of her locker when Heidi came in.

Heidi smiled in her usual quiet, awkward way. She opened the locker next to Yasmin's. "You did a good job. It must feel good to know you had the winning shot."

Yasmin smiled up at her. Heidi was taller even than most of the boys at their school. It made sense that she was their center.

"Yeah, thanks!" Yasmin said. "I think I did pretty awesome too. So did you! We all did."

She was feeling gratified—like Coach had seen how good she was and wanted to reward her. He'd put her in the starting lineup as soon as she'd arrived at Dexter less than a month ago. And he had let her play all the way through the game.

She knew she had work to do—she had to work on her layups, for one thing. But that was fine, she could do that. Her mom, dad, and coaches had always said it was good to know what you needed to improve. It helped you form a plan. They also said it was important not to beat yourself up.

Instead of feeling tired, she already felt energized to start practicing layups.

"I think I did pretty awesome too," a mocking voice said behind her.

Yasmin turned. Kelly Holgar was reaching into her locker further down the row. She pulled out her clothes, frowning.

"Why do you always have to brag like that, Yasmin?" Kelly said. "Always talking about how *awesome* you are. We don't talk like that on this team, and no one wants to hear it."

"Brag?" Yasmin stood holding her towel, confused. "That's not bragging. I'm just—"

"I mean, who gave you the assist?" Kelly went on. "You wouldn't even have made that shot if it wasn't for me."

"But I still made the shot," Yasmin shot back. The words were out before she could stop them.

"We play as a team and win as a team," Kelly said. "There's no 'I.'" She looked Yasmin up and down. "Maybe it's different where you come from. Speaking of, where *do* you come from? Maybe you should go back there. Forever. This is our country."

Then she walked away, her bag slung over her shoulder.

Yasmin stared after her. She felt her face redden. She cleared her throat, but her voice came out husky.

"What's she talking about?" she asked.

Heidi watched Kelly leave too, her mouth hanging open. Then Heidi said softly, "Come on. Let's hurry up and get out of here."

CHAPTER 2

NOT IN HOUSTON ANYMORE

Heidi and Yasmin changed their clothes quickly. Yasmin couldn't remember the last time she'd wanted to get out of a locker room so fast. Her heart was pounding and her thoughts raced.

She hated these feelings. Usually, she felt like she could do anything.

Yasmin followed Heidi out onto the school lawn. Parents waited in cars lined up at the curb. She was glad to see that her mom wasn't there to pick her up yet.

Yasmin wanted a moment to talk to Heidi alone. She had two questions. The first one seemed easier to ask.

She cleared her throat again, but her voice seemed to have vanished. Finally, she was able to speak. "Why'd she say I was bragging?" she asked. "We *did* do awesome."

Heidi tucked a strand of blond hair behind her ear. "I don't know," she replied. "I guess around here, people don't really talk about it when they do a good job. There's nothing wrong with it, but I guess we just don't do it."

Yasmin could hardly believe her ears. "*That's* what she's upset about?" Yasmin cried. "She's mad that I said I did awesome? I did! So did everyone else on the team!"

Heidi nodded. "I know. Like I said, you don't usually hear people say it out loud." She shrugged. "Don't worry about it. I think it's kind of cool to show you're proud."

Yasmin suddenly missed her old school in Houston, badly. It was hard to believe it had only been a month since her family had moved to this small town in Michigan.

Back home, her friends and teammates would rib each other all the time. They'd joke around and make fun of each other. But they were super proud of each other too. Whenever she said she'd done a great job, her teammates would joke and agree—and it never bothered anyone.

"That's the dumbest thing I ever heard," Yasmin mumbled. "What's wrong with being confident? It shouldn't be a problem."

Heidi waited, like she knew Yasmin was about to ask something else too.

Yasmin swallowed as she built up her nerve. She had to ask now or she'd never get it out.

"And . . . ," she started slowly, "what do you think Kelly meant about going back to where I came from, and that this is her country?"

Heidi shuffled her feet. "I think . . ." She bit her lip. Yasmin could see it was hard for Heidi to talk about too, but it was important. "I don't think she meant going back to Houston."

It was the answer Yasmin was afraid of. Her stomach sank.

"I can't believe it," Yasmin said. "She actually said something racist to me."

"Has that ever happened to you before?" asked Heidi.

"No," Yasmin said.

Her mom was from India and her dad was white. Yasmin's skin was brown, but at her old school that hadn't been a big deal at all. There were tons of kids in every shade of brown you could imagine. Her friends were Asian, Latinx, Indian, Black, Native American, everything.

Here, Yasmin had definitely noticed that she was the only brown kid on the basketball team. She was only one of a few kids of color in her whole grade.

There were two Black kids, an Asian kid, and her. But until now, she didn't know it would be a problem.

Heidi looked embarrassed. Her head hung down and her eyes focused on the ground. "I'm sorry that happened," she said. "I can't believe she said that. She was in the wrong."

Yasmin sat down on the brick wall next to the school sign. She trembled in a weird way she never had before. Of course, she'd heard that some places were still like this. But she'd never been able to imagine it.

"Just because she feels like that doesn't mean other kids will," Heidi said.

"But everyone listens to kids like her," Yasmin said.

Heidi didn't say anything, probably because she knew it was true. Everyone on the team seemed to like and respect Kelly. All the teachers did too. That had been obvious to Yasmin from the very beginning: Kelly was a straight-A student, super polite to all the

17

teachers, into sports and academics, on the student council, and all about school spirit. The exact kind of kid teachers loved.

A car honked.

"Oh, sorry . . . that's my dad," Heidi said. "I gotta go. See you tomorrow." She paused. "I hope you're OK."

Then she headed off to her dad's car, her shoulders hunched. Yasmin realized Heidi walked like that everywhere except on the court. There she held her head high.

Yasmin slumped on the wall and wondered if Heidi would talk to her tomorrow. Heidi was as blond and pale as you could get. What if she turned out to be like Kelly and decided it was too much trouble to talk to the new kid who looked different? Was Yasmin going to be completely alone at school and in basketball?

Yasmin's mom's car pulled up to the curb. Yasmin picked up her bag and walked in slow motion.

As soon as she slid into the seat, her mom asked, "What's wrong?"

There was no fooling her mom. She'd just keep badgering her with questions until Yasmin gave in and answered. So Yasmin decided to be direct and just blurt it out.

"This girl just said something racist to me," she said, slumping down into her seat.

Her mom's hands tightened on the steering wheel as she pulled away from the curb. "I'm so sorry, honey," she said.

Usually, her mom had warm and comforting things to say. Today, though, she pressed her lips together as she drove. "I was hoping it wouldn't happen," she said finally.

"But you thought it might happen?" Yasmin said. All the anger she felt at Kelly rose up in her chest. "Why didn't you tell me? You could have warned me. Then maybe I would have felt more prepared."

"I hoped it wouldn't, but you never know. This

area is different from Houston in many ways. I've experienced it a couple times already at work too." Her mom grimaced. She was a doctor and had gotten a job at the hospital.

"No one's said anything to me directly," she added, "but some patients and nurses have made a bigger deal than they needed to about where I'm from. It's not always obvious, but you know it when it's happening. Sometimes it's just ignorance, and sometimes it's more than that." She shook her head. "I'm sorry, Yasmin."

"Why'd we have to move to this stupid town, then?" Yasmin said. "Especially if you knew it might be like this?"

Her mom didn't answer, because she knew that Yasmin knew why. They'd moved because of her dad's job. He'd gotten an amazing opportunity at a company nearby. It was too good to pass up, so they'd packed up and moved here.

"We'll talk to Dad about this, and figure out a strategy," her mom said. "It's not OK for anyone to talk to you like that." She patted Yasmin's hand. "Don't worry, we'll figure it out."

Yasmin slumped even further down in her seat and glared out at the street. "Well, I wish we'd never come."

CHAPTER 3

MAKING A PLAN

When they got home, Yasmin went outside to practice. The first thing her dad had done when they'd moved was install a hoop over their garage, and Yasmin used it every chance she could.

She launched into her layups—first, two-foot layups, planting her feet right, getting enough balance and power to explode upward toward the basket. Again and again and again, trying to blow off steam.

Her rage coursed through her as she burst upward to shoot, keeping her form solid. She moved into one-foot layups, keeping her right hand and right leg in smooth motion.

Usually shooting baskets helped center her. It helped her stop focusing on problems and start working toward solutions. It wasn't working for her now, though. She shot again and again, but it wasn't making her feel a whole lot better. She just wanted to punch something.

She started practicing dribbling instead. She worked on her footwork, her pivots, crab dribbles, step back and sidestep, between cross, retreating. Then she started freestyling, fast as she could, the ball thwacking the concrete driveway.

She stopped, panting and sweating. It was the only time she could remember when shooting hoops didn't help calm her down.

She went back inside, up to her room, and closed the door. She paced back and forth across her floor. Kelly's words just kept running through her head. The sting wouldn't go away.

She'd never been so angry—or so shaken—in her whole life.

She decided to video chat her best friend, Louise. Louise was back home in Houston, where Yasmin should be.

Louise hadn't seen Yasmin cry that often, but Yasmin started crying as soon as her friend picked up the phone. Louise was sitting in her familiar bedroom with the pink plaid curtains and the orange palm tree lamp. Just two weeks ago, Yasmin had been with her, eating popcorn in that bedroom.

"Yasmin! What's wrong?" Louise exclaimed. "Did you lose a game?"

"No!" Yasmin sniffled. "I've never cried because of a game."

"Then what is it?" Louise asked. "Did you get in a fight with your parents? Are you having problems making friends?"

"No, nothing like that." Yasmin shook her head. She caught her breath and calmed herself down.

25

Finally, she said, "This girl said something racist to me today. And Mom said some people at the hospital were weird to her already too. I hate this place. I want to come home."

Louise listened to her talk for more than fifteen minutes.

"I wish you could come home too," Louise said finally. "We miss you. The team's not the same without Three-Point Jones."

Yasmin smiled.

"But since I'm pretty sure you are stuck living there, you'll have to show them they can't mess with you," Louise said.

"I will," Yasmin said.

By the time Yasmin got off the phone, half of her felt better. The other half felt worse.

There was a knock, and her dad poked his head into her room. "Come on down and eat, Yasmin. Mom told me what happened."

Reluctantly she went downstairs. She doubted her

parents would really understand how she was feeling. She sat down and started picking at the casserole Dad had made, not wanting to eat. Her parents both looked tired and worried.

"I hate this place," Yasmin announced. "I want to leave."

"I'm sorry about what you experienced, honey," Dad said. He was trying to hide it, but he looked almost guilty, like he knew if it weren't for his job she wouldn't be going through this.

Yasmin had all kinds of new, unfamiliar thoughts running through her head.

"No one would ever talk to *you* like that," she told him.

Her dad's skin was pale. People never treated him differently because of how he looked—he fit in everywhere. She glanced over at her mom, who had deep brown skin. Then, Yasmin studied her own hand. Her skin color was somewhere between both her parents' colors, but she was definitely brown.

There was no way anyone would ever think *she* was white.

She hated that she was having all these thoughts. But one of them popped out before she could stop herself.

"I don't get it," she said. "There's this kid named Darius in my grade. His dad's from Iraq and his mom's white. But *his* skin is lighter than mine. He pretty much looks white. No one talks about him. At least, I've never heard anything in the month I've been there."

Her mom looked more and more upset. "Your skin is lovely the way it is," she said. "And you never know how people's skin will turn out when you have mixed races." She sighed. "Yasmin, we want to help you come up with strategies for dealing with this."

"How about moving back to Houston?" Yasmin said.

Her dad shook his head. "We're going to give this place a shot, at least. I don't think leaving is a reasonable solution," he said. "But if you run into someone who's ignorant about race, we want to help you be prepared to get through it. You're not alone with this."

"Also remember that so far, it's only been one ignorant girl," her mom said. "Most of the other kids likely don't feel that way."

"They *might*," Yasmin said glumly. "Maybe they just aren't as rude as Kelly, so they don't say it to my face."

"She shouldn't be saying things like that to anyone, even if she doesn't know any better," her mom said.

Yasmin picked at her food. "No one would believe that she said it. She's perfect."

"She's clearly not perfect if she's treating other students that way," her dad said. "I'm going up to the school to talk to your teachers tomorrow."

"No!" Yasmin shouted. "You can't do that!"

Her dad put his napkin down. "Why not?"

"Because then everyone *will* hate me, for sure!" Yasmin sat up straighter. "Please, Dad. Just let me deal with it."

Her parents looked at each other.

"All right—for now. If it happens again, we're going up there, though," her mom said. "No one should be treating you that way."

Yasmin nodded. She managed to swallow a few bites of food, then went upstairs and got ready for bed. She crawled under her covers, but she couldn't fall asleep right away. Usually, right before she went to sleep, she'd have good thoughts. She'd think about the game and her friends and what she was going to do that weekend.

Tonight, all she could think about was whether the same thing would happen tomorrow and if the other kids felt like Kelly did.

Louise's voice rang through her head: *You'll have to show them they can't mess with you.*

I will show them, Yasmin decided. It was the only

way she could take care of this by herself. She'd *prove* to Kelly—and all the other kids who thought like her—that they couldn't bring her down.

She finally felt a little better. She fell asleep with her fists curled up.

CHAPTER 4

READY TO CONQUER

Yasmin got to school super early the next morning and practiced on the outdoor courts. She loved early mornings for shooting hoops, when no one else was around. She felt herself go into the zone: her attention narrowed and it was just her and the ball.

She worked on her jump shots, trying to find the perfect shot pocket. She did her best to get rid of the hitches and to avoid two-motion shots. She loaded her shot pockets lower, making sure her legs and the ball went up at the same time. She wanted the jump shots smooth.

She clenched her jaw. *She was going to do this.* She was going to be the best at jump shots, free throws, layups, all of it. She'd be the best at everything and earn the respect of the whole team. And then girls like Kelly couldn't say a word to her.

By the time the first bell rang and she had to go to class, she felt better. Her jump shots had improved. She felt strong.

During lunch, Yasmin found a seat in the cafeteria near the corner. She was staring into space, eating a carrot, when she heard, "Can I sit here?"

Yasmin looked up. It was Heidi, standing in front of her with a tray.

Yasmin glanced around the bustling cafeteria. "Oh, sure," she said.

As Heidi sat down, Yasmin realized how relieved she felt. Apparently, Heidi hadn't decided to hate her after all.

"Are those jelly donuts?" Yasmin asked, pointing to Heidi's lunch.

Heidi nodded as she opened her lunch bag. "Yeah. Want one?"

As she took a donut, Yasmin realized she had questions for Heidi but didn't know how to ask them. Heidi was so quiet—she never seemed to talk about her family or anything. And she didn't seem to hang out with a lot of people. She was kind of a loner.

But before Yasmin could ask her anything, something small came sailing through the air and landed on her tray. She jumped in her seat, then poked at whatever it was: a crumpled piece of paper.

She looked around, but no one seemed to be looking at her. She couldn't tell who'd thrown it.

Heidi looked worried. "Let's eat somewhere else."

But Yasmin had already opened the paper. Inside was a note scrawled: *Go back to where you came from. No one wants you here.*

She dropped the note. Her cheeks flamed red.

Heidi reached for the note and read it, her face turning pale.

"I gotta go." Yasmin hurried from the cafeteria out into the hallway.

Heidi dashed after her, still holding the paper. She handed it to Yasmin. "You should tell someone," Heidi said. "And show them this. It's evidence. Go tell Principal Higgins." Heidi pointed. "Her office is right down there. I'll go with you."

Yasmin turned and walked down the hall with Heidi, numb. She had only met the principal once, when she'd first enrolled. Principal Higgins seemed nice enough, but she couldn't tell much beyond that.

The principal's office door was closed. Yasmin lifted her hand to knock, but stopped.

"What's wrong?" Heidi said.

Yasmin hesitated. She knew her mom and dad would want her to tell. But they didn't get how it was in middle school. Even at her old middle school, which was pretty great, there was still bullying and kids who always felt left out.

She dropped her hand. Every place had rules for

fitting in, even if no one talked about them. And she didn't know the rules of this place yet. If she told on someone as popular as Kelly, the other kids would hate her for sure. Then she'd have no chance at all. They'd call her a snitch forever. Or worse.

Yasmin stepped back from the door. There were better ways to do this. She was Three-Point Jones, after all. Three-Point Jones didn't let people get the better of her—she got even.

"I have a plan instead," she said, spinning around. "I'm going to deal with this on my own."

"I really think you should tell," Heidi said.

"Trust me, they won't mess with me anymore once I show them," said Yasmin.

She headed back into the hallway. As she passed the other students, her head raced with suspicions: which one of these kids had thrown the note? It might have been Kelly, but it could have been someone else too. How many of them felt the way Kelly felt and just weren't saying it?

CHAPTER 5

SLAYING AT PRACTICE

By the time Yasmin got to practice, she was angry again. And ready to slay in a way she'd never been before. She had so much adrenaline that she couldn't stand still. She'd show these people. She'd be better than all of them if she had to be. Her layups and jump shots had already improved. There was no reason she couldn't be the best at all of it.

Before she sprinted out onto the court, she texted Louise.

Going to show them on the court today!

Louise texted back. *You go, girl!*

Yasmin smiled. It was good to have loyal friends.

She darted out onto the court. Kelly and her little circle of friends giggled as she passed them. But instead of shrinking away, Yasmin went up and dribbled inches away from them, startling them. Then she streaked across the court before they could say a word.

"Get on the line!" Coach called.

Time for running drills. Coach always had them do full-court runs. She sprinted to the free-throw line and came back, to the mid-court and then back, to the opposite free-throw line and back, and then the length of the court and back.

Yasmin sprinted like her life depended on it. She decided she'd be faster than ever before—and she was. She streaked past everyone else, hurtled to the mark, turned on a dime, raced back.

"Great speed, Yasmin—but take it easy, this is just a warm-up!" Coach shouted.

She never thought she'd hear Coach say something like that.

"Nope, I can keep going," she panted without breaking her speed.

She was on fire. Back and forth, back and forth. *I just have to show these guys I'm meant to be here.*

Coach moved them into the shooting drills. Yasmin took a deep breath as she took shot after shot, flicking her wrist to get good rotation on the ball. Then, Coach had them line up to practice dribbling the ball into the key one by one, while another player played defense.

On Yasmin's turn, she charged toward the girl guarding her—Leah Sonberg, tall and strong. *I won't let her shake me.* Yasmin faked like she was going left. As soon as Leah moved that way, Yasmin went right. Leah recovered, got closer again. Yasmin turned to play post and Leah moved behind her. Yasmin accidentally threw her elbow back too far and stepped back so fast that Leah stumbled.

"Boom!" Yasmin shouted, as she whirled around to make a jump shot. Leah was still staggering back.

Coach shook his head. "Back of the line, Yasmin! You fouled her."

Yasmin muttered to herself but went to the back of the line. She held her head up, even as she heard Kelly and another girl whispering.

When Coach moved them into half-court five-on-five, Yasmin and Kelly were put on opposite teams. The rule was that if the ball changed hands, they had to walk it out to the free-throw line. Kelly dribbled. Yasmin was guarding her. Kelly dribbled slower and higher today than usual, and it looked like Yasmin would have the chance to steal the ball. She knew she might get another foul if she tried, but it was a chance to show them what she was made of.

She went for it, knocking the ball out of Kelly's hands—but accidentally hitting Kelly's wrist at the same time.

"What's your *problem*, Yasmin?" Kelly shouted.

"Foul!" shouted Coach. He blew his whistle. "OK, girls, cool down!"

They lined up again for cool-downs—stretches, lunges, ankle rotations. Yasmin stretched as far as she could without hurting.

"That's it for today!" Coach called. "Good practice. See you at the game on Saturday!"

Everyone slowly drifted off the court. Yasmin heard laughter. She turned to see Coach laughing at something Kelly had just said. Her stomach sank. It definitely looked like Kelly was one of Coach's favorites too.

Coach caught her eye. "Yasmin, come talk to me for a minute."

Yasmin followed Coach to his office, ignoring the snickers from Kelly and her cronies. She wouldn't let them see that she was nervous, even if her insides were about to melt. She made sure the office door was shut behind them. The last thing she wanted was for the others to hear him chewing her out.

He leaned back against his desk and folded his arms. "Great speed and power today. But what else is going on? You seem angry."

Coach was super blunt, which Yasmin usually appreciated. But she couldn't bring herself to speak, so she looked at the floor. It felt weird not to answer—she'd never been anything but totally honest with her coaches.

"I just want to remind you," Coach said, "that there are two types of players—those out just to make themselves shine, and those who want to lift up the whole team. I want you to be the second kind. Got it?"

"Kelly said something racist to me," Yasmin blurted out. "She told me to go back to my own country."

Coach's expression changed. His eyebrows knit together. She couldn't tell if he was angry. She held her breath, waiting.

"That doesn't sound like Kelly," he said, sounding confused.

"Well, she did," Yasmin said. "I wouldn't make something like that up. And yesterday someone threw a piece of paper at me in the cafeteria that said, 'Go back to where you came from.'"

His expression became even more confused. "Are you accusing Kelly of that too?"

"*No*. I didn't say that." She felt heat rise up in her chest. Why was he acting like she was making things up?

Coach kept looking confused. "I just don't know what to think. Kelly's a good student and great team member. It's very hard to imagine that she'd do those things."

Yasmin stared at him. She couldn't believe it. She felt like she was going to be sick.

"Never mind," she said and got up.

She left quickly, shaking. For the second time in two days, she was more upset than she'd ever been.

CHAPTER 6

DEALING AT DINNER

At home that night, Yasmin dragged her fork through her food again. She had no appetite.

"What's wrong?" her dad asked.

Yasmin sighed. She'd been wondering what to tell her parents. She was sure if she told them about the note and that Coach hadn't believed her, they'd storm the school, demand answers, and cause a fuss. And now that she knew how Coach felt, she figured the other teachers probably felt the same way.

It seemed like everyone in this town had known each other all their lives. They'd just think Yasmin was jealous of the school star.

She decided to be vague about it. "It's still a little weird," she said carefully.

"Give the other kids time," her mom said. "People have to get used to what they don't know. I'm hoping the teachers will provide some guidance and education too."

"And listen, Yasmin," her dad said, "we can look into other schools if this continues to be a problem. I don't want you to stay at a school that treats its students badly. We'd probably be able to find another school, maybe a private one, with more diverse students and faculty."

Yasmin stared at her plate. Another school in this town might be just the same. "I just want my old school," she said glumly.

"I know," her mom said, and patted her hand.

Yasmin thought of how Coach had probably

told all the other teachers already that she was making things up. Maybe they would all hate her by tomorrow.

She took a bite of chicken. "I just want to *show* Kelly and the others they can't beat me."

Her mom smiled. "Sounds like a plan. But remember you don't need to prove anything to anyone, Yasmin."

She went back to her plate. How could she tell her parents that she had everything to prove, to everyone?

CHAPTER 7

THE DANCE

Their next practice ended with lots of footwork—dribble tag, jump rope. Yasmin jumped until she felt like her heart would explode. Side-to-side jumps, forward to backward, jogging-in-place jumps, single-leg hops. She jumped until she felt it in every part of her body.

As she doubled over, panting and trying to catch her breath, Coach said, "Just a reminder that I want all of us at the Fall Dance tonight. Having the team there is good for school spirit. So, we're going to help with the decorations in the gym, head home to change, and then head back here."

Yasmin didn't mind that Coach had volunteered the team for helping with the dance decorations. She *did* mind that they were being forced to attend the dance. Of course, Coach had already sent emails out to the parents about that. That morning Yasmin's mom had said, "Exciting! Maybe you'll meet some nicer kids there."

"Doubt it," Yasmin had grunted.

Her old middle school had dances too, and she hadn't loved those much either. It was a bunch of kids standing around, drinking fruit punch and dancing awkwardly with about two feet of space between each other, and teachers who looked stressed out the entire time.

She had a feeling this one would be even worse. Reluctantly, she helped blow up balloons and hang streamers and sparkly signs that said *Dexter Middle School Fall Dance*. The only thing that kept her going was the thought that maybe she could rile Kelly up a little bit somehow.

When the decorations were done, Coach called out, "OK, head on home to get changed!"

At home, Yasmin changed into one of the three dresses she owned. Then her mom drove her back to the school, fussing over her more than she usually did.

"Remember to call us if anything goes wrong," she said as she dropped Yasmin off.

Yasmin shuffled into the gym. Even though she'd been there just an hour ago and had hung some of the decorations herself, the gym still looked amazingly transformed. Students poured inside, looking way nicer than they had at school that day.

She glanced around and saw Kelly standing with a bunch of friends. She went in the opposite direction, weaving past people dancing, all the way to the back wall. Her science teacher, Mr. Blake, was manning the refreshments table. He was almost completely hidden behind an enormous bowl of fruit punch.

Yasmin found a safe spot along the wall near the table. From there, she stared out at the sea of people. She wasn't feeling quite as bold about riling Kelly up as she'd planned, which bugged her. Kelly was currently laughing and joking with Coach. Yasmin's stomach sank. Had Coach even tried to talk to Kelly about what had happened? It didn't look like it. She and Coach looked as chummy as ever.

Kelly glanced over at Yasmin, met her eyes for a second, and turned to say something to her friends. A few of them glanced over too, then went back to talking among themselves.

Yeah, it definitely didn't seem like Kelly had gotten a talking-to.

Yasmin's stomach dropped even more. She scanned the gym, looking for the easiest route to get out of there. She could call her mom and tell her she had a stomachache. She was about to make a beeline for the door when she noticed someone on the other side of the table, also pressed against the wall.

It was Heidi. She was watching everyone else too.

Yasmin went over to her. "Sorry if I was rude earlier," she said. She hated apologizing, but she also knew it was important. Her least favorite thing—besides Kelly—was people who didn't apologize when they were wrong.

Heidi was wearing a long blue dress. She gave a little half smile. "It's OK."

Yasmin leaned against the wall next to her. "So, no dancing?"

Heidi snorted. Yasmin smiled. She'd never heard Heidi do or say anything sarcastic before.

"Nah," Heidi said. "Who'd dance with me?"

Yasmin was even more surprised. "What do you mean?"

Heidi turned to look at her. "They make fun of me too, you know. It's not the same as racism, but it still sucks."

Yasmin was surprised that Heidi had said it so bluntly, without blinking.

"No guy wants to dance with a girl way taller than him," Heidi went on.

Yasmin wanted to correct her and tell her she was wrong. Then she realized that, unfortunately, she might be right. Middle school boys were weird about lots of things.

"Maybe we'll all be the same height by the time we're in high school," Yasmin said.

Heidi shrugged and smiled. "I like being tall. *I* don't have a problem with it."

"Good," Yasmin said. Then she frowned. "I don't know if I like this school. My old school was way better."

Heidi nodded. "I can see why. It sucks to feel different."

Yasmin clenched her fists. "It's stupid that some people have to feel different."

Heidi nodded. "And it sucks that certain people are jerks. Hey, did you catch the Lakers game on Friday?"

Yasmin smiled. "No, I missed it. I heard it was great!"

As Heidi talked, Yasmin felt the tiniest bit lighter. Maybe not everyone at Dexter Middle School was awful.

She and Heidi spent the rest of the dance by the wall, talking about basketball, movies, and music. By the time the dance was over, Yasmin realized she'd had fun—and not because she'd danced.

She'd officially made a new friend.

Louise was excited when Yasmin texted her the news. *If I wasn't worried about you at that school, I'd be jealous.* <3

For the first time in a while, when Yasmin got into bed that night, she felt like there might be some hope.

CHAPTER 8

DEFEAT

The next away game was against Anderson Middle, which had one of the best teams in the region. Yasmin had been excited to play them. But as their team's bus pulled into the Anderson parking lot, her palms wouldn't stop sweating. She was more nervous than usual.

The one good thing, though, was that nothing else had happened—no more notes or confrontations from Kelly. Yasmin finally felt like she could focus on the game.

The team trooped into the school and went to put their stuff away. As Yasmin unzipped her gym bag to put her water bottle inside, she saw it: a crumpled pink Post-it note.

She hesitated for a moment, wishing it would disappear. Wishing it away.

Finally, she picked it up and said, "I can't believe it. Another note. And right before a game."

"What?!" Heidi stepped closer. "What does it say?" She looked over Yasmin's shoulder.

Yasmin opened it slowly. Her hands were shaking. Holding the note so Heidi could see too, she read to herself.

Tell your whole family to take you back to where they came from.

For a second, Yasmin felt like she couldn't breathe. She stood there in shock. *Is this how it's going to be? Am I always going to worry about racist notes appearing in my bag or locker? Am I always going to have to worry about some racist comment?*

Finally, she crumpled the note and hurled it across the locker room.

Heidi ran to grab it. She smoothed out the note and stuck it back in Yasmin's bag.

"That's *evidence* and you need to hang on to it," Heidi said. "Just like the other one. Don't get rid of it! You've got to tell Coach."

"He won't believe me or care," Yasmin said abruptly. "I already talked to him once and he didn't do anything."

Heidi raised her eyebrows. "You didn't tell me that."

"I don't even know if Kelly's the one who did this," Yasmin said.

Coach blew the whistle to gather the team. Yasmin put her gym bag in the locker and shut it.

"I still think you should tell," Heidi muttered as the girls headed out for the court.

Yasmin felt less steady on her feet than usual. Usually, she liked to bound out onto the court, but today she felt stiff and halting. She couldn't focus. Who had written the note? When had they snuck it into her bag?

She tried to gather her thoughts and make herself focus. If she just kicked butt out there on the court—if she could be Three-Point Jones—she'd finally win the respect of her team.

It felt doomed from the start. As soon as Dexter got possession, Yasmin started trying get open to take a three-point shot. She tried all her old tricks: faking, getting the defender to jump, and then sidestepping with a dribble and trying again. For some reason, she came up short.

Her shot banged off the front of the rim. The next time she tried, she managed to get enough arc on the shot. But it rolled off her pointer finger— and she missed again. The ball bounced off the backboard.

"What are you *doing*?" Leah shouted at Yasmin during the second quarter. Yasmin had just shot her fifth unsuccessful attempt from beyond the three-point line.

By then Yasmin was in full-on panic mode. How could this be happening? She was known as Three-Point Jones. Yet these shots were sloppy and awful.

But she felt desperate. She *needed* to earn her old nickname back, and earn the respect of her teammates. How else was she going to get them to stop making fun of her?

In the last quarter, Anderson had a six-point lead. She could give it another try. If she just made two three-pointers, she'd get Dexter back into the running. It was her chance.

But Coach called a time-out. "Listen, Yasmin," he said, "I want you to focus on passing. That's your job for the rest of the game—I want you to pass to other players. Got it?"

She nodded numbly. Her embarrassment grew and grew. She was so glad her parents weren't there to see this game.

She started passing, and Dexter started to catch up. Kelly and Heidi made shots. By late in the last quarter, Anderson was only up two points.

The Anderson point guard dribbled past Yasmin, coming from the opposite side of the court. Yasmin followed. If she could just get possession, she could pass to Heidi or Kelly. One of them could shoot from inside the key—and they could get in the final shot for their team. The others would see she was a great team player and accept her.

Yasmin lunged after the point guard, knocking the ball from her hands. And accidentally tripping the girl.

"Foul!" shouted the ref.

It was a dumb mistake that happened at the worst possible time. Yasmin couldn't even look at her teammates, but she felt their rage.

Silently, she watched the Anderson player take two free throws. She made both shots. Just like that, Anderson was up by four.

With only seconds left, there wasn't enough time for Dexter to make up the difference.

Applause for Anderson rang through her ears.

Yasmin turned and walked off the court, her head pounding.

CHAPTER 9

PLAYING IT SMART

Usually, when a player messed up that badly, teammates said at least *something* supportive to her.

Not this time. On their bus ride back, no one said a word to Yasmin, except for Heidi and Coach. Heidi slipped into the seat next to her as Yasmin stared out the window and stewed.

As the bus headed back across town, Coach told them all they'd done a great job. Then he lumbered to the back of the bus and sat across the aisle from Yasmin and Heidi.

"Don't beat yourself up. I know you meant well. It's all right," he said in a low voice, so the rest of the bus couldn't hear. "Next game, let's work on impulsive moves and playing it smart."

Yasmin closed her eyes and nodded. She knew that for the next few days, she'd be replaying every single mistake she'd made on the court that day— every misfire, every bad move.

"I've messed up lots of times," Heidi said quietly, after Coach had gone back to the front of the bus.

"Probably never this badly," Yasmin said. "I *really* didn't need another reason for anyone to hate me."

* * *

At practice the next Monday, Coach called the team together before warm-ups.

"Time to change our starting lineup!" he called.

Yasmin froze. "Why?" she blurted.

"So that everyone gets a chance to play," Kelly snapped.

"We rotate twice a month," Coach said. "So, we're changing it up today, and we'll give the new starters time to practice together. Sound good?"

The girls who were now going to be starting cheered. Yasmin tried to hide the fact that she wanted to sink through the floor.

"This isn't how it was at my old school," she whispered to Heidi. "Our best people were the starters."

Heidi shook her head. "Not every school is the same. It's nothing personal. You just happened to start here right when we had a rotation."

Yasmin wanted to believe that it wasn't personal, but she couldn't quite make herself. As the new starting center, point guard, shooting guard, and forwards practiced together, Yasmin went up to Coach.

"Are you sure this isn't because of what happened at the last game?" she said.

"No, it's nothing personal," he said, echoing what Heidi had told her. "We do this regularly."

That only made her feel a little better. She couldn't imagine what her old team would say if they saw her on the sidelines now. She ran through her drills robotically, still trying to focus on her three-point shots. She hoped no one was laughing at her as they watched her practice them.

After practice, she dragged herself back to the locker room, trying to ignore the sinking feeling in her stomach. As she walked in, she saw someone near her locker.

The person was slipping a piece of paper inside.

"Hey!" Yasmin called.

The girl turned. It was Kelly. She hurried away and was out of the room before Yasmin could say anything else.

"I saw it too," Heidi said, coming up behind Yasmin.

Yasmin ran to her locker, opened it, and found the

paper. This one said, *Hope you enjoy your trip back to your home country.*

"Go tell Coach," Heidi said. "I'll back you up and tell him I saw it too."

"He won't believe me," Yasmin said. "I told you, he loves Kelly. He'll think we're lying."

"Then tell your parents," Heidi said. "You have to. She can't get away with this. What if she does that to someone else?"

Yasmin took a deep breath. Heidi was right—this was more important than worrying about whether the team would hate her.

"Will you come with me?" she asked Heidi.

Heidi nodded. "Of course."

CHAPTER 10

TELLING

She'd never been so nervous to tell her parents anything. She made them all go into the living room and sit on the big, squishy couches so they'd at least be comfortable. Heidi sat next to her in the recliner. Having Heidi there gave her courage.

"Honey, what is going on?" her mother said, confused.

Yasmin took a deep breath and then told them everything. This time, she didn't leave anything out. She told them about the notes, about telling Coach, about how Coach hadn't believed her, and about how she'd chickened out about telling the principal.

Her parents' eyes got bigger and bigger as she talked. When she was done there was a huge silence. Then both her parents started talking at the same time.

"I can't believe it," her mom said. She was near tears. She stood up and came to hug Yasmin. "I'm so sorry, honey. Why didn't you tell us more of this sooner?"

"I was scared the whole team would hate me if you got involved," Yasmin said. "I wanted to deal with it myself."

"Your safety and peace of mind are what matter most," her dad said. "This is unacceptable." He turned to Heidi. "You saw this girl put a note in Yasmin's locker too, Heidi?"

Heidi nodded. "Yes," she said quietly. "And I was there the first time she said something to Yasmin too."

Her mom sat back down. "I'm so glad you found the courage to tell us now."

Yasmin felt tears prick her eyes. She hated to cry, but she remembered that Louise always said it was good to cry. Louise was a fan of crying. Yasmin let herself take that advice for a minute.

"We're going to go in to speak to the principal tomorrow," her dad said. "And we'd like you there, of course, Yasmin. And you too, Heidi, if you'd be willing to come."

Yasmin glanced at Heidi. "Are you all right with that?"

Heidi smiled. "I'd be glad to."

* * *

Principal Higgins's office was cold and official-looking. There was a big wooden desk and diplomas all over the walls. There were also framed photos of a lot of the school's sports teams.

Yasmin's mom, her dad, and Heidi sat next to her on the other side of the principal's desk. Yasmin's mouth was dry.

"So, what can I do for you?" Principal Higgins asked.

Yasmin froze up when she saw that some of the framed pictures were of the school's basketball teams. One of them was for a basketball championship from a few years ago.

Yasmin swallowed. What if the principal was just like Coach? What if she loved the school's basketball team so much that she wouldn't hear a word against one of its stars? What if she thought Yasmin was just a liar.

Her mom squeezed her hand. "Go ahead and tell her," she said. "And be thorough."

Yasmin took a deep breath. Then she told the principal everything. It was getting a little easier for her to talk about. The principal's eyes also got wider and wider, just as her parents' had.

Yasmin pulled out the notes she'd been given and laid them on the principal's desk. She pointed. "That's the last note Kelly left me."

Principal Higgins's face was pale. "And this is Kelly Holgar, from the basketball team?"

"Yes," she said nervously.

"I assure you my daughter isn't making this up," her mom said.

"She's not," Heidi said quietly. "I was right there when she told Yasmin to go back to her own country. I heard her say it. And I was there when she put the latest note in Yasmin's locker."

The principal grew even paler. "I'm so sorry. This is unacceptable. Yasmin, I truly believe that this is a rarity at our school. But even one instance is too much. We will take action. Have you spoken with Coach about this?"

"Yeah, but he didn't seem like he believed me," Yasmin said, still nervous. "He just acted like I was 'accusing' Kelly. I don't know if he ever talked to her about it, but I don't think he did, because she kept acting the same."

Principal Higgins looked even more troubled. "I'm very sorry to hear this. I'll speak with him right away. This isn't the type of thing we want at our school at all."

"I'm scared she'll tell the basketball team that I told on her, and then they'll hate me even more than they did after the game," Yasmin blurted.

"You still did the right thing by coming to me," Principal Higgins said. "Racist actions and language are completely unacceptable. It will be up to Coach to tell other students that racism is not tolerated here at all. That's the grown-ups' job to ensure that."

"Thank you for taking this seriously, Principal Higgins," her dad said. "We appreciate it. We want our daughter to feel safe at school."

"I'll speak with the coach and with Kelly today," said Principal Higgins, gathering some papers together. "And I'll be in touch about all this. Thank you all for trusting me with this. And again, Yasmin, I'm so sorry. You're very welcome at our school."

Yasmin glanced at Heidi. Heidi smiled at her, and she smiled back.

CHAPTER 11

TEAMWORK

Things were pretty quiet before their next game, which was at Brasher Middle. They didn't have another practice before then, and Yasmin only saw Kelly a couple of times in the hall. Both times, Kelly avoided her.

The day of the game, Yasmin was stretching in the locker room when Heidi joined her.

Heidi moved into a lunge. "You nervous?"

"Yeah," Yasmin admitted. "But not as bad as before." She had to admit she felt a little lighter since they'd gone to see the principal. "I still don't know if the team will be weird with me."

"Just remember that you did the right thing," Heidi said. Then her eyes got wide. "Hey—I think someone wants to talk to you. She's walking toward us. I'll see you in a minute."

She left suddenly. As soon as she disappeared, Kelly came close to Yasmin.

"Hey," said Kelly nervously. She stopped and shifted on her feet. "So . . . I'm sorry for those notes. It was wrong and I shouldn't have done it."

Yasmin studied her. It was obvious someone had told Kelly to apologize, and that she was only saying sorry because she'd been forced to.

"As long as you stop saying and writing racist things to me," Yasmin said. She looked Kelly in the eye. "But are you sure you're not just going to get your friends to take over for you?"

Kelly turned red and looked down. "I won't," she mumbled.

"Good, because I'm tired of dealing with it," Yasmin said. "No one should have to deal with it."

Kelly nodded abruptly, turned, and walked away. Yasmin watched her go.

She realized she felt even lighter inside than before. She knew Kelly had probably been told she'd get taken off the team if she didn't apologize. They would probably never be friends. But maybe if Kelly valued the team that much, and Yasmin did too, they could find a way to work together—as teammates. And that was all Yasmin wanted.

They did their pregame huddle, Coach gave them their pep talk, and then the starters bounded out onto the court. Yasmin sat down and waved to her parents in the stands. Her mom's beautiful brown face stood out in the crowd.

It was a strange experience to have to sit down to watch the others play. Yasmin jiggled her foot as she watched. They hadn't played Brasher before, and it turned out Brasher was great at offense. They started off with possession and had the score at 12–6 only halfway through the first quarter.

By the end of the first quarter, both Dexter's new starting center and the shooting guard—Jess Mitchell and Brianne Harwick—were already lagging. Brasher was tiring them out.

Coach went to talk to the ref, then called Jess and Brianne out and put Heidi and Kelly in. Yasmin watched them both bound out onto the court. It was obvious they were delighted to be out there.

Her foot jiggled harder.

Heidi was amazing—a great rebounder and great on defense in general, keeping the other team from gaining the advantage. And Kelly was so small and fast that she could weave between players. She would steal the ball before anyone realized she'd done it and dart to the basket in the blink of an eye.

Yasmin had never realized it before, but now, watching from the sidelines, she realized how well their team worked together. They were seamless, like they were all sharing a brain. No one stood out more than the others; they were all good.

Late in the fourth quarter, Coach called out the point guard, Nicola Stevens. Then he came up to Yasmin. "Want to go in?" he asked.

She leaped to her feet. "Yes! Oh my gosh! Of course!"

"Good. And before you go, Yasmin—I'm sorry," Coach added. "I shouldn't have ignored what happened to you. We'll talk about it more later, but I want to assure you that I'll listen to your concerns from now on."

She stared at Coach. This apology felt real. He truly looked sorry.

"Thanks," she said.

"Good. Now go do what you do best! You've got this!" Coach yelled.

She hurried out onto the court. With only five minutes left in the game, she found herself near the three-point line in possession of the ball. The Dexter supporters in the crowd started chanting: "Shoot! Shoot!"

"I'm open!" Kelly shouted.

Kelly was near the basket. The girl guarding Yasmin was on her like glue. Yasmin wasn't confident she'd make the shot.

Three-Point Jones would have gone for it anyway. Her old admirers would have been disappointed in her. For a second, she felt the old fear: what if she was no one at all—if she wasn't the star?

Then her head cleared. She was Yasmin Jones, basketball player. Point guard.

She passed to Kelly, who caught it, spun around, and leaped into one of the smoothest layups Yasmin had ever seen.

The Dexter crowd went wild. There was no time for Brasher to recover.

She saw her parents stand up in the stands, cheering. Heidi came over and hugged her as the rest of her team jumped up and down.

After the game, Yasmin's mom and dad rushed up to her. They gave her a huge hug and hugged Heidi too.

"You were amazing!" her dad said.

Yasmin laughed. "I was barely in it! But I did do a pretty good job passing."

"You did a *great* job passing," her mom said.

"That's what really mattered," added Heidi.

"I'm curious—why didn't you go for it?" said her mom. "You could have made that shot, Miss Three-Point Jones."

"I want to learn to work more as a team," Yasmin said. "That's important too."

She turned and watched Kelly and Leah and the others hugging their families too. Whatever happened, the solution might not be perfect. Kelly might start up again one day, or another kid might. But Yasmin had spoken up. She'd stood up for herself. And she was learning to be a team player. Her game was only getting better.

Coach made his way over to her parents. "Hi, you're Yasmin's parents? I'm Coach Hargrave."

"Hi," said her parents. Yasmin could tell they were surprised.

"I just wanted to let you know I've spoken to the principal, and I want to say how sorry I am for not addressing Kelly's racist actions," said Coach. "I should have taken Yasmin seriously. No student should have to deal with racism. I've spoken with Kelly, and I'll definitely be looking out for Yasmin in the future. She's a great player and a great kid."

"Thank you, Coach," said her mother. "That means a lot."

"I've got to go talk to some of the other parents, but please reach out if you have any questions," said Coach. He gave Yasmin a high five, then bustled off.

Yasmin looked at her parents, amazed. "He said sorry and meant it!" Yasmin said.

"Some grown-ups are good at apologizing," her mom laughed.

Yasmin felt about a hundred pounds lighter.

"I think this calls for ice cream," her dad said.
"Heidi, would you like to join us?"

Heidi and Yasmin smiled at each other.

"I'd love to," Heidi said.

ABOUT the AUTHOR

Salima Alikhan has been a freelance writer and illustrator for fourteen years. She lives in Austin, Texas, where she writes and illustrates children's books. Salima also teaches creative writing at St. Edward's University and English at Austin Community College. Her books and art can be found at www.salimaalikhan.net.

GLOSSARY

adrenaline (uh-DREH-nuh-luhn)—a chemical the body produces when a person is excited, causing the heart to beat faster and giving more energy

assist (uh-SIST)—a pass that leads to a score by a teammate

center (SEN-tur)—position on a team usually held by the tallest player

dribble (DRIH-buhl)—to bounce the ball with one hand

key (KEE)—the marked area on a basketball court surrounding the basket

layup (LAY-up)—using one hand to push the ball up and bounce it off the backboard and into the basket

point guard (POYNT GARD)—position on a team that runs offense and makes sure the ball gets to the right player at the right time

post (POHST)—a player who is comfortable playing with his or her back to the basket

racist (RAY-sist)—cruel or unfair treatment of people because of their race

shooting guard (SHOOT-ing GARD)—player on a team whose main job is to score points and steal the ball on defense

DISCUSSION QUESTIONS

1. It was important to Yasmin to prove to her new team that she was a really good player. As the story goes on, why does this become even more important to her?

2. Yasmin was afraid to tell the principal or her parents what had really been happening. Why do you think it was so hard for her to be honest?

3. By the end of the story, Yasmin discovers something about teamwork. What does she learn?

WRITING PROMPTS

1. Yasmin thought of herself as Three-Point Jones and was proud of how good she was at shooting three-pointers. Name something you do really well and write about it.

2. Yasmin was treated differently at her new school for looking different. Write about a time you didn't fit in with a group. How did it feel? How did you handle it? Compare your experience to Yasmin's.

3. When Yasmin first told her coach about what Kelly had done, he didn't believe her or take her seriously. Write about a time you needed someone to believe you. How did you handle it?

MORE ABOUT BASKETBALL

Basketball was first invented in 1891 by James Naismith, a teacher at a YMCA in Springfield, Massachusetts. He created the indoor sport to keep young athletes busy and healthy during the cold months.

The first basketball "hoops" were actually just peach baskets with the bottoms intact, and the first backboards were made of wire. Officials had to get the ball out after each basket.

When basketball was first invented, dribbling wasn't allowed. The moment players caught a ball, they had to throw it to another player. In 1897, dribbling became part of the game.

In the early 1900s, basketball players would play in cages of chicken wire and mesh so that they wouldn't fall into the spectator seats.

In 1904, Black gym teacher Edwin Henderson decided to teach Black students basketball. At that time, Black athletes were not allowed to play sports with white players. This continued through the early 1900s. Henderson hoped basketball would help bring about racial equality and help Black students get into white colleges in the North. Basketball eventually caught on in Black communities.

In the early to mid-1900s, before Black players were allowed to join the National Basketball Association (NBA), dozens of all-Black basketball teams formed around the country. They called themselves the Black Fives. Often, the Black Fives would offer basketball and dance at their events to bring in crowds. People would come to watch games and dance to ragtime music.

When the NBA was formed in 1946, it didn't allow Black players. In 1950, 21-year-old Earl Lloyd became the first Black player to play in an NBA game. As the United States slowly changed, Black athletes were finally recognized. Black players helped turn the sport into what it is today.

FOR MORE AWESOME
ACTION ON THE COURT,
PICK UP . . .

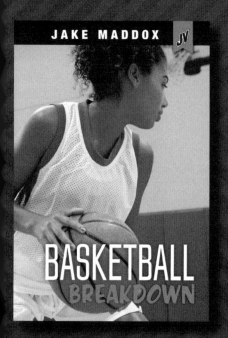

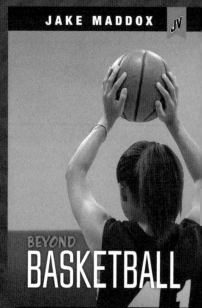